Dear Parent:
Your child's love of reading starts here!

Every child learns to read in a different way and at his or her own speed. You can help your young reader improve and become more confident by encouraging his or her own interests and abilities. You can also guide your child's spiritual development by reading stories with biblical values and Bible stories, like I Can Read! books published by Zonderkidz. From books your child reads with you to the first books he or she reads alone, there are I Can Read! books for every stage of reading:

SHARED READING
Basic language, word repetition, and whimsical illustrations, ideal for sharing with your emergent reader.

BEGINNING READING
Short sentences, familiar words, and simple concepts for children eager to read on their own.

READING WITH HELP
Engaging stories, longer sentences, and language play for developing readers.

READING ALONE
Complex plots, challenging vocabulary, and high-interest topics for the independent reader.

ADVANCED READING
Short paragraphs, chapters, and exciting themes for the perfect bridge to chapter books.

I Can Read! books have introduced children to the joy of reading since 1957. Featuring award-winning authors and illustrators and a fabulous cast of beloved characters, I Can Read! books set the standard for beginning readers.

A lifetime of discovery begins with the magical words **"I Can Read!"**

Visit www.icanread.com for information on enriching your child's reading experience.
Visit www.zonderkidz.com for more Zonderkidz I Can Read! titles.

ZONDERKIDZ

Bubblegum, Maps, and Missing Patience
Copyright© 2012 Big Idea Entertainment, LLC. VEGGIETALES®, character names,
likenesses and other indicia are trademarks of and copyrighted by Big Idea
Entertainment, LLC. All rights reserved.
Illustrations © 2011 by Big Idea Entertainment, LLC.

Requests for information should be addressed to:

Zonderkidz, 5300 Patterson Ave SE, Grand Rapids, Michigan 49530

ISBN 978-0-310-73283-9

LarryBoy Meets the Bubblegum Bandit ISBN 9780310721611
Bob and Larry's Creation Vacation ISBN 9780310727316
Bob and Larry and the Case of the Missing Patience ISBN 9780310727309

Editor: Mary Hassinger
Art direction: Karen Poth
Cover design: Diane Mielke
Interior design: Ron Eddy

Printed in United States

13 14 15 16 17 18 /DCI/ 8 7 6 5 4 3 2

LarryBoy meets The Bubblegum Bandit

Hands that work hard will rule.
But people who don't want
to work will become slaves.
— Proverbs 12:24

story by Karen Poth

One day, Mayor Blueberry
saw something strange.
The Bumblyburg Elementary
School was a mess!

She tried to find the janitor.

But all she found were mops

hanging in the closet.

When she found the janitor, he was
just standing in the messy hall.
"Something must be wrong,"
Mayor Blueberry thought.

The halls were a mess.

There was gum stuck to the walls.

But she could not be late.

She was going to a big swim meet.

Outside, Mayor Blueberry

saw Spud, the yard boy.

His mower was not mowing.

His rake was not raking.

Spud was lying in a hammock.

He was reading a book

and chewing gum.

"Something must be wrong,"

thought Mayor Blueberry again.

At the pool, the swim team was

not ready for the meet.

They were not even in the pool.

"We don't feel like swimming
today," said Laura Carrot.

Something was very wrong.

The whole town was lazy!

Mayor Blueberry called LarryBoy.

RING, RING!

At the LarryBoy mansion,

Alfred answered the phone.

"Master Larry, it's the mayor.

There is an outbreak

of laziness in the city."

LarryBoy did not hear Alfred.

He was reading a comic book

and eating a donut.

He was dropping crumbs

on the floor. What a mess!

In fact, his whole room was a mess.
LarryBoy's clothes and toys
were everywhere.

"Master Larry, what are you doing?

Bumblyburg needs you!"

Alfred said.

"Oh, Alfred," LarryBoy said.

"I just don't feel like being

a superhero today."

"Master Larry," said Alfred,

"God doesn't want us to be lazy."

"Oh, okay, Alfred," LarryBoy said.

But his super suit was as

big a mess as his room.

Alfred pulled a hanger off

LarryBoy's back.

"Master Larry," he said,

"this hanger is stuck with … gum!"

"Oh, yeah," LarryBoy said.

"I got this jar of golden gum balls

from my new friend, Bubba."

"Have some," LarryBoy continued.

"They're yummy!"

Looking wrinkled and torn,

LarryBoy jumped into the Larrymobile

and headed to the mayor's office.

While he was gone, Alfred grabbed the
gum and got to work on his computer.

When LarryBoy got to the
mayor's office, Bubba was there.
He brought some gum balls for
the mayor, the police chief,
and Editor Bob too!

"Would you like a gum ball?"

Bubba asked politely.

As LarryBoy took the gum,

Alfred burst through the door.

"Spit out your gum!" Alfred shouted.

"Oh, Alfred," LarryBoy said,

"I didn't get the flavor out yet."

"LarryBoy, this is serious!"

Alfred said.

"Your new friend is not a friend.

He is a villain named 'The

Bubblegum Bandit!'

To break his lazy spell,

everyone in Bumblyburg

must spit out their gum!"

Alfred's words made Bubba mad.

He began to get bigger and bigger.

"He is blowing up like a bubble,"

said LarryBoy.

"We have to stop him."

He launched his super-suction ear.

The wrinkled, torn suit didn't work.

LarryBoy was stuck to

the bad bubble!

"Everyone spit out your gum!"
Alfred yelled.

As they did, the bubblegum villain
began to shrink.

He got smaller and smaller.

Soon he was nothing

but a wad of gum

stuck to LarryBoy's ear.

"I think it is time to clean my

super suit,"

LarryBoy said with a smile.

Bumblyburg was saved!

Thanks to ... LarryBoy!

Hands that work hard will rule.

But people who don't want

to work will become slaves.

— Proverbs 12:24

God saw everything he had made.
And it was very good.
—Genesis 1:31

 I Can Read!™ BEGINNING 1 READING

Bob and Larry's Creation Vacation

story by Karen Poth

Bob and Larry love to go on vacation.

This year, Larry has planned

a special trip.

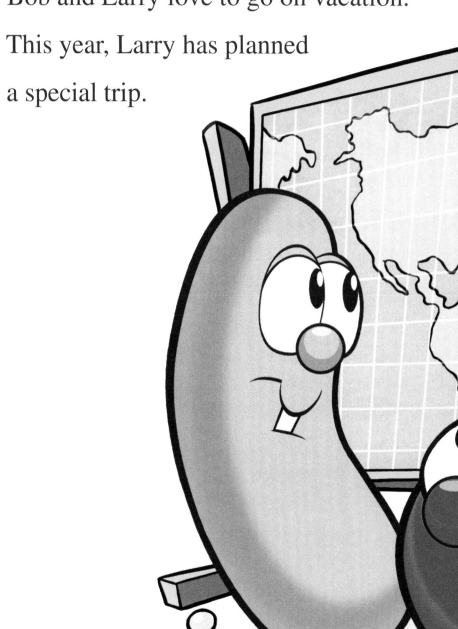

"We are going
to see all of
God's creation!"
Larry told Bob.
The two friends
looked at a map.

"We can't do that," Bob said.

"We don't have enough time."

"Sure we do," Larry said.

"We only need seven days!

Pack your bags," Larry said.

"We leave in the morning!"

"On the first day,

God made the light," Larry said.

Bob and Larry sat on the beach.

They enjoyed the light.

It was a good day!

"Later on that same day," Larry said, "God made the night." Larry turned out the light.

Then Larry started to snore.

It was a better night for Larry

than for Bob!

"On the second day," Larry said,

"God made the sky!"

Bob and Larry flew

like birds in the sky!

It was a good day!

"On the third day," Larry said,

"God made the blue sea!"

Bob and Larry swam in the ocean.

It was a good day!

"Then later, on that same day,"

Larry said, "God made the land."

"It is good to be on land!"

Bob said, happy to be out of the water.

"On the fourth day,"
Larry said,
"God hung the sun,
moon, and stars."

"They give the world more sparkle,

don't you think, Bob?"

Larry asked.

It was a good day!

"On the fifth day," Larry said,

"God made the fish

in the water."

"And the birds in the air!" Bob said,
as a pelican picked him up
and flew away.

It was NOT a good bird!

"God made more than
    10,000 kinds of birds," Larry said,
"and more than 28,000
    kinds of fish!"

God worked hard on day five!

It was a good day!

"On the sixth day,"
Larry said,
"God made the creatures
on the land."

"All of them," Bob said,

"from the littlest ant

to the biggest elephant!"

"Think about all the creatures

God made that day!" Larry said.

"Bugs and rabbits, turtles and deer,

beetles and mice, starfish and owls."

"And later that same day," said Larry,

"God made man and woman."

"He named them Adam and Eve!" Bob said.

It was a good day!

On the seventh day,

Bob and Larry were tired!

They had seen all that God created.

So just like God, they decided to rest!

It was a GREAT vacation!

God saw everything
he had made. And
it was very good.
—Genesis 1:31

Be kind and tender to one another.
Forgive each other, just as God forgave you ...
—Ephesians 4:32

I Can Read!™

Bob and Larry in
The Case of the
Missing
Patience

story by Karen Poth

Welcome to the City Detective Agency.

This is Bob and Larry.

They are GREAT detectives.

Bob carries his badge.

Larry carries his stuffed badger.

The badger helps Larry be brave.

One day, Bob and
Larry were teaching
a SWAT class.
Chief Nezzer came in.
He brought three new
detectives.

"This is the Pod Squad," Nezzer said.

"Teach them to be great detectives."

Bob and Larry were glad to help.

71

RING!

Bob picked up the phone.

Mrs. Carrot had seen the

Masked Door Slammer!

Bob and Larry had been looking

for the Door Slammer for weeks!

They had to hurry.
"Come on," Bob said
to the Pod Squad.
But they did not all
fit in Bob's car.

They took the Pod Squad's van.

Oh no! About halfway there,
the van stopped working.
The detectives were stuck!

Bob and Larry pushed the van.

The peas sang songs.

By the time they got to the scene of the crime, the Door Slammer was gone. "Sorry, fellas," said Mrs. Carrot.

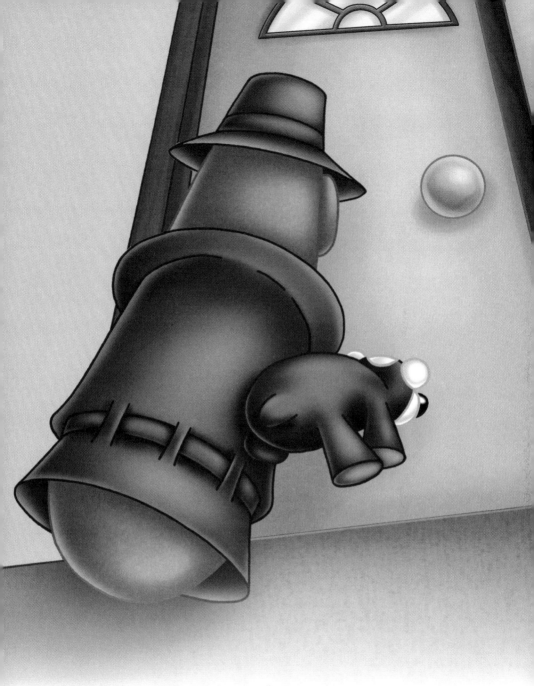

She closed the door.

"Rats!" said Larry.

"Looks like we missed him again!"

"This is your fault," Bob said
  to the Pod Squad.

"Yeah," said Larry, "and now
  we have to walk home!"

Bob and Larry hurt the
Pod Squad's feelings.

On their way back
through the park,
the detectives came
upon another crime!

"It was a bicycle!"

Madame Blueberry said.

"It knocked over my

hot dog cart and kept going!"

A trail of mustard led

Detectives Bob and Larry

to another crime!

The bicycle had ruined

Pa Grape's wet cement too!

This Bicycle Bandit had to be stopped!

Bob turned to the Pod Squad.

But the peas had fallen down a hill.

They were covered in yellow

police tape.

"Can't you do anything right?"

Bob asked.

The detectives followed the

bandit's trail.

It ended in Scooter's backyard.

They found the Bicycle Bandit!

It was Lil' Pea!

"Why did you do it?" Bob asked.

"Hold on," the Pod Squad said.

"We don't think this little fella
is a criminal."

Just then Laura Carrot ran

into the yard.

"It's all my fault!" Laura shouted.

"I was teaching Lil' Pea

how to ride his bike.

"He did everything wrong.

I said mean things and I pushed him!

I'm sorry, Lil' Pea. I wasn't very nice."

Then Bob realized something.
He and Larry had done the same
thing to the Pod Squad.

He and Larry were supposed to

teach the Pod Squad.

Instead they got angry with them.

"We're sorry," Bob said to the Pod Squad.

"Yeah, God wants us to use nice words
  and encourage one another," Larry said.

Bob and Larry spent the

rest of the day teaching

the Pod Squad to be great detectives!

A man's wisdom makes him patient.

He will be honored if he forgives someone

who sins against him.

—Proverbs 19:11